Monster Math

Written by **Anne Miranda** Illustrated by **Polly Powell**

Voyager Books · Harcourt, Inc. SAN DIEGO NEW YORK LONDON

www.HarcourtBooks.com

First Voyager Books edition 2002
Voyager Books is a trademark of Harcourt, Inc., registered in
the United States of America and/or other jurisdictions.

The Library of Congress has cataloged the hardcover edition as follows:
Miranda, Anne.
Monster math/written by Anne Miranda; illustrated by Polly Powell.
p. cm.
Summary: A counting book in which a little monster's
birthday party gets out of control.
[1. Monsters—Fiction. 2. Parties—Fiction. 3. Birthdays—Fiction.
4. Counting. 5. Stories in rhyme.] I. Powell, Polly, ill. II. Title.
PZ8.3.M657Mo 1999
[E]—dc21 98-12933
ISBN 0-15-201835-2
ISBN 0-15-216530-4 pb

E G H F

The illustrations in this book were done in gouache and pen and ink on illustration board.
The display type was set in Fontesque.
The text type was set in Elroy.
Color separations by Tien Wah Press Limited, Singapore
Printed and bound by Tien Wah Press, Singapore
Production supervision by Sandra Grebenar and Wendi Taylor
Designed by Lori McThomas Buley

For Bill Pistone,
brother-in-law and dear friend

—A. M.

For all the monsters in the Powell clan, with love

—P. P.

One little monster is looking at you.

There's a knock at the door . . .

and now there are two.

Three silly monsters can stand on their heads.

Four bouncy monsters are jumping on beds.

Five screaming monsters are chasing each other.

Six wiggling monsters are posing for Mother.

Seven starved monsters are licking the dishes.

Eight blow out candles and make birthday wishes.

Nine sticky monsters are washing their faces.

Ten speedy monsters run ten monster races.

The monsters keep coming and Mother's lost count.
Ten more make twenty—a monstrous amount!

Thirty loud monsters are dancing and singing.

Now there are forty! The doorbell keeps ringing!

Good grief—there are fifty! That's really too many.

Guess who is wishing she didn't see any?

She shoos away forty....

Ten monsters won't budge.

Five wave good-bye. Five monsters make fudge.

Another departs.

Four monsters are leaping.

One leaves the house. Three monsters are creeping.

At last two go home and the party is done.
How many are left? Could there be only...

one?

The house is a wreck and the couch has been frosted.
The food's been devoured and Mother's exhausted.

But one little monster is grateful and glad.
It's the best birthday party that she's ever had!